CODA

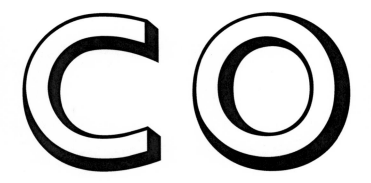

{*A Novel*}

René Belletto

Translated by Alyson Waters | Foreword by Stacey Levine

UNIVERSITY OF NEBRASKA PRESS | LINCOLN AND LONDON

© 2005 Editions POL.
English translation
and foreword © 2011 by
the Board of Regents of
the University of Nebraska.

Cet ouvrage, publié dans le
cadre d'un programme d'aide
á la publication, bénéficie du
soutien financier du ministère
des Affaires étrangères, du
Service culturel de l'ambassade
de France aux États-unis, ainsi
que de l'appui de FACE (French
American Cultural Exchange).

This work, published as part of a
program providing publication
assistance, received financial
support from the French Ministry
of Foreign Affairs, the Cultural
Services of the French Embassy in
the United States and FACE (French
American Cultural Exchange).

French Voices Logo
designed by Serge Bloch.

Library of Congress
Cataloging-in-Publication Data
Belletto, René. | [Coda. English]
Coda : a novel / René Belletto;
translated [from the French]
by Alyson Waters ; foreword by
Stacey Levine. | p. cm.
"Winner of the French Voices Award."
ISBN 978-0-8032-2441-4
(paperback : alkaline paper)
1. Experimental fiction.
I. Waters, Alyson, 1955– II. Title.
PQ2662.E4537C6313 2011
843'.914 — dc22 | 2010014495

Set in Electra by Kim Essman.
Designed by Nathan Putens.

FOREWORD | *Stacey Levine*

The forward-looking French Voices translation series has been a boon and a pleasure for many North American readers, from devoted followers of contemporary currents in French fiction to those who find these books by chance. This translation of René Belletto's *Coda* continues the program and University of Nebraska Press's enriching practice of bringing lively, provocative literary works to a new audience.

Belletto is known in France as a literary-thriller author whose works are marbled with characteristics of detective, noir, and science fiction genres. In one of his translated novels, *Eclipse* (*L'Enfer*), a depressed musician learns of a criminal's plot to kidnap a child, and to intervene he kidnaps the child himself. In *Machine* (*La Machine*), a psychiatrist invents a mechanism that switches brain impulses between two human bodies, so that he can literally experience the mind of another. American reviewers received both these works in the 1990s with praise.

Coda was an outlier among Belletto's works, French critics suggested when the book was published in France in 2005. Its style, subject matter, and central conceit broke the Belletto mold. The book is certainly a strange jewel, simultaneously spoofish, artificial, comic, and philosophical, with a hermetic sensation about it. Moreover, the text refuses to spell out for the reader the extent to which it commits to any of these values. The result, as readers will see, is to Belletto's credit: *Coda* is a work that hovers mysteriously on the border between reality and artifice, natural and supernatural. The story is a puzzle, too, and so lingers in the mind.

It begins with a startling, over-the-top proclamation by the novella's unnamed narrator: "It is to me that we owe our immortality, and this is the story that proves it beyond all doubt." *Coda*'s twisty, humorous, nearly hyperbolic plot then lets us know how this has come to pass. The abrupt, suspect appearance of a package of frozen seafood in the unnamed narrator's freezer, his meeting with an old school friend, the appearance of Marthe, a spectral, strangely behaving woman who walks into the school friend's cocktail party without having been invited — all these events render the narrator puzzled and out of sorts. Finally, made intensely anxious by an apparent kidnapping, he speeds through the countryside, seeking (he believes) to save his daughter's life before the novella's climactic final scene.

There is something humorous about the narrator of this text. His blithe taste for luxury goods, his aplomb, and the expansiveness of his voice stand in contrast to the strange and precipitous events that occur around him; even when he is at his most desperate, he seems somewhat detached. Perhaps in this narrator, Belletto is satirizing all hapless protagonists in all adventure novels.

Yet Belletto's unnamed protagonist has some special and characteristic traits. With the help of his father, he has built an almost-perpetual motion machine, which is the book's central motif. The machine, made of steel balls, wheels, and wires, remains in motion for some time, but its performance is not truly perpetual. After twenty-four hours, the system runs down.

Within the plot sequence, characterizations, and other machinery of this tale, I think, lie some fundamental human questions: Why can't time be extended or reversed? Why can't I live forever? How can I somehow remain with those I love? *Coda*, like the machine it describes, ends exactly where it begins, creating a circular loop. And inside the loop, Belletto has given those fundamental questions a most original treatment.

From her lovely, delicate hands
I take the book, and I look.

RENÉ BELLETTO, *Coda*

I

It is to me that we owe our immortality, and this is the story that proves it beyond all doubt.

. . . . . .

On Monday, the first of August in the year _ _ _ _ at 9:30 a.m., Anna and I arrived in front of the Parc Monceau in Paris. I was bringing my daughter to the house of her maternal grandparents, Maurice and Maureen Michelangeli.

She was to spend most of the month with them.

. . . . . .

The Michelangelis had always taken good care of Anna, especially since the death of her mother a year and a half earlier.

I believe that, could they have done so at the time, they would have kidnapped her without hesitating for a second.

They had despised me from the start. By marrying Maria, hadn't I stolen their only child from them, and wouldn't they have wanted to take their revenge by stealing Anna from me?

I don't say this lightly. I know for a fact that they suspected me of having murdered Maria; they had even gone so far as to hire a private detective to look into what I'd been doing on the night of the murder.

No, I was not with Maria (alas, I was not with her!) on that March night when a stranger followed her through the hallways of the big house in Versailles where we were living and shot her in the back several times — a thief (who stole several valuable objects), an assassin and a madman, not a trace of whom was found, ever.

Fortunately, Anna was sleeping at her grandparents' that night.

The detective must not have uncovered anything suspicious about me. He didn't come to see me a single time, and I never heard of him again. But I have proof he was investigating me.

As the months passed, I began to hope that the Michelangelis had put their monstrous suspicions out of mind.

. . . .

Maria used to love listening to the Spanish singer Juan Valderrama (who died, I learned with sadness, last April). In one of his songs, Valderrama says the name "Anna Maria" in such an enchanting way that, when Maria was pregnant, she told me if we had a daughter she wanted to name her Anna.

Anna, beautiful little angel, was born exactly six years to the day before this story begins.

She had her mother's dark curly hair and resembled her in every way except for her mouth, which was shaped just like mine. I'm sure Maurice and Maureen were put out by this;

they would go into raptures over Anna's every feature except her mouth.

Did they love Anna? I'm not sure. I don't think I could say they didn't. Perhaps what they loved best in her was their daughter. Still, their attitude was affectionate; they never tried to turn her against me, and Anna, denied her mother's company, was happy in Maureen's.

. . . .

We were to come home on July 31, but Anna had wanted me to drive at night so she could sleep in the car, a real treat for her. I informed the Michelangelis of our plans, and we left the Brunnen Hotel at nightfall.

We drove straight through from Cologne to Paris.

I woke Anna to give her a first birthday kiss at the stroke of midnight, at the exact moment when July 31 became August 1.

At 8:00 in the morning, having returned to Paris without incident, we arrived at Rue Mademoiselle, where we packed Anna's bags.

She took advantage of our stop at home to start up our perpetual motion machine — four little balls that needed to be placed on a cogwheel.

Her suitcases were ready.

I knew the Michelangelis were eager to have Anna. I had promised to bring her to them on the 1st, after our short trip to Cologne.

On the 5th, they were to take her for about three weeks to Saint-Haynaut-le-Haut, a little spa town near Clermont-Ferrand. Maurice and Maureen had both had kidney problems a few years earlier. They had recovered, but they continued to take the waters of Saint-Haynaut every summer because their doctor advised them to do so, and because they had grown fond of the pretty village and the Massif Central and its volcanoes.

. . . .

Maria had been a specialist in her field and often participated in conferences and colloquia abroad. Ten months after we were married (she was then seven months pregnant), I traveled with her to Cologne and was awed by the cathedral's massive proportions.

Anna, too, went into raptures when she saw how high the towers rose. She'd raised her arms to the sky and looked at me as if for me to confirm that the towers indeed soared to such heights. (What grace, what life in her gesture, and in her pure smile of a goddess discovering our planet!)

For the last week of August we had planned a short vacation in Morón de la Frontera, the city in Andalusia where Maria had been born by sheer chance: before retiring from business, the Michelangelis had been constant travelers, and they happened to be in Morón when the baby came, well before she was due.

Anna was looking forward to this trip to Spain. She was thrilled about it well ahead of time.

She adored "Juanito" Valderrama, whose songs had soothed her since her earliest childhood.

She had not become a fragile and gloomy little girl in whose presence one avoided speaking about her mother. The seemingly serene way she lived with that horrible memory remained a mystery to me.

4

Avenue Marguerite is a private residential street about three hundred feet long that connects Boulevard Malesherbes to Parc Monceau. Flanked by tall trees, the street appears to be part of the park, but in fact there is an impassable railing dividing them at the far end.

At 9:30 a.m. I parked my long black Phénix Maxima (definitely the most beautiful model ever to come out of the Phénix factories) in front of number 9.

The Michelangelis' house, the last one on the left, was an enormous neogothic edifice, remarkable for its corner turrets and its many gabled dormer windows. You went in on the avenue side, but the main façade overlooked the park, so that from the inside you felt more like you were in a castle in the heart of a forest than in the middle of a big city.

Both Maurice and Maureen had come from well-to-do families. Already rich when they married, they later inherited an international food processing business. They turned out to be good managers and amassed yet another fortune. As they got older, they grew weary of world travel and had become homebodies, rarely leaving Paris except for their yearly vacation in Saint-Haynaut.

Lorima stroked Anna's cheek.

"You look tired, sweetheart!"

Lorima, whose hair was white despite her youth, had been working for the Michelangelis for six years and lived with them.

"It's just from having spent the night in the car," I said. "After her nap, she'll be as good as new."

Lorima smiled. Anna was famous for how soundly she slept at naptime.

Anna's grandparents showered her with birthday presents. Even Lorima gave her a very lifelike little metal lamb. Nothing, however, made her as happy as the outrageously expensive watch I'd put on her wrist the previous evening at an inn near Cologne where we'd dined. She admired it constantly, and she made everyone else admire it.

There was no question of sitting down to a meal with the Michelangelis to celebrate Anna's sixth birthday. That gives you some idea of how well we got along.

I left shortly afterward.

I kissed Anna, my *gente et belle demoiselle*, good-bye and headed for my 11:30 appointment with Dr. Mateau.

Hervé Mateau was a G.P. who had been practicing for a long time in my neighborhood, on Rue Notre Dame. He had moved to Rue de Lourmel to be closer to his new girlfriend, who lived on Rue du Théâtre.

He'd got the results of my lab tests. My hemoglobin levels were still too low, whereas the other results were all normal; this was the mystery. Now Mateau wanted me to consult one of his friends, Dr. Luis Moreno, a hematologist who would perform a myelogram. He called him right away. Moreno wanted me to come in on Thursday, August 4, at 3:00 p.m. He would pierce my sternum and remove some bits of bone marrow that would then be analyzed. "Just to be on the safe side," Mateau said to me. But I wasn't worried; I didn't feel ill.

Coincidentally, Luis Moreno was the son of Luis Moreno, the famous hematologist from Lyon who, along with Dr. Suig of the Suig Clinic, had saved the life of my uncle Manuel's daughter, my cousin Michèle. In just one night, Suig and Moreno had destroyed the microorganism that had been attacking my cousin when she was a child.

At 12:30 p.m., I glumly downed three heavy crepes in a restaurant on Rue de Lourmel. I dreaded the month of August as it stretched to infinity before me, dreaded Anna's absence, dreaded solitude, a solitude I both feared and longed for and that had tormented me since Maria's death.

I thought of my dear friend Albin de Vil, who was dead as well. How I missed him!

I was eager to get out of the restaurant. The television, with its usual spectacle of a world careering toward its end at breakneck speed, was deafening. And I hadn't noticed that the coffee in my cup was almost boiling; I burned my lips and left the place on edge.

I did some shopping nearby. I had nothing left in the house. My refrigerator was empty. I piled up all kinds of groceries on the back seat of the Maxima and went home.

I had sold the house in Versailles right after Maria's death.

Anna and I now lived at 6 Rue Mademoiselle, in Paris, on the ninth and last floor of an ultra-luxury building whose final touches were just being put on when we moved in. On the street side, the enormous apartment opened out on a 1,600-square-foot balcony with a garden of grass and dwarf trees.

On certain days when the wind was right, we could hear the distant, muted sounds of the church bells from Place Notre-Dame-des-Monts.

I had to make two trips from the car to the elevator to bring in all my bags, and then two more trips from the elevator to my apartment.

I was exhausted from the sleepless night, but I knew I wouldn't be able to close my eyes. I sat down on my black leather couch in the living room, facing my array of gigantic audio speakers, and I remained thoughtful.

And then I got up again. I had to put away the frozen food.

I went into the kitchen, walked toward the fridge, and opened the freezer.

And then . . .

But before I recount the event that was simultaneously ordinary and unbelievable, and that thrust me so directly into this story, I think I need to clear up a few things about my affluent lifestyle.

My parents, since they had nothing, left me nothing.
This statement is not entirely true.

. . . .

My father had spent the war as a prisoner in a labor camp.
At night he would escape into his thoughts, dreaming up the
perpetual motion machines he would build when he got out
and that, through the fame and fortune they would bring him,
would pull him out of the hole into which the various tribula-
tions of his life had plunged him. Of course, he was well aware
that perpetual motion did not exist, that no mechanism could
function autonomously and create energy without any outside
source. But his faith, nourished by so many hours and years of
despair, was strong — and it survived the war.

When he returned home, over time he built seven of the
eight systems he had invented.

Nothing perpetual, alas, except inertia.

The eighth and cleverest (for although his ideas were naïve,
they were nonetheless those of a true inventor) was the one in

which he believed the most. Not only had he put off making it, but in the end he had given up on it entirely, for financial reasons, he told me, and because the prototype's fabrication had to be entrusted to tool and die specialists and he was afraid his idea would be stolen.

Still, the real reason lay elsewhere. I understood (and he confessed to me) that he was afraid of yet another failure — an irrevocable one this time — and he preferred to carry his dream of eternity with him into his eternal rest.

Although he knew I never shared that dream, shortly before his death he said to me:

"You try when I'm gone!"

I promised I would.

. . . .

One evening in January _ _ _ _ , I went to Albin's father's house. I had become close to Maurice de Vil since his son's death, and he was in my opinion the man for the job. I told him the story and showed him the sketches my father had left me, meticulously drawn with genuine grace in the lines.

He agreed to handle everything.

As was expected, no perpetual motion machine came of this. Nevertheless, with capable design engineers, first-class materials, and perfect fittings, the system of spirals and cogwheels my father had imagined ran for an entire day, twenty-four hours. Four steel balls coated with rubber drove the wheel whose movement made the spiral turn, and the spiral, by the very fact of being a spiral, raised the balls to the summit from where they would tumble to the top of the wheel, and so on. After twenty-four hours, the system would run down, and if you didn't want it to stop completely, you had to put one of the balls back on the cogwheel. For this reason — and for several others, including the small amount of energy it produced — the machine had no practical application.

I couldn't help but be disappointed.

How could I better meet my father's expectations?

In small five-and-dime stores in working-class neighborhoods, I'd often enjoyed seeing those mock aquariums in which electricity created the illusion that a photograph of a maritime scene was a real, three-dimensional seascape in miniature, choppy waves and all. One night, as my thoughts were drifting, I had a vision of a luxury product that would combine a marvelous "aquarium" with our perpetual motion machine. The machine would provide the requisite electricity and, at the same time, it would in itself be a very original decorative piece.

I put the idea to Maurice de Vil. It was convincing enough for him to have the project studied.

I'll skip over the various production stages. Two years later, our system was selling very well in several countries. A significant factor in its success was the way young children were fascinated with the perpetual motion machine, spiral and wheel, even more than with the aquarium: they never tired of watching the balls go up one side and come down the other, and they were quite content to reset the balls when the mechanism was about to stop.

Maurice de Vil managed the business, relieving me of all worries. All I had to do was collect the payments made to me each quarter.

Albin had been an only child. I'd met him in high school, and we had gone to college together.

Our passion for music united us.

We had transcribed several pieces of early music for two guitars. Our goal was to play them in concert for one or two years and then record them. Unfortunately, we overestimated both our energy and our talent: the concerts exhausted us, and experience taught us we were not good enough as instrumentalists.

We gave up (while continuing to play together for our enjoyment) and devoted ourselves to another project dear to us, the compiling of an etymological dictionary that was to be both concise and useful to the greatest number of people.

A short while ago, when we had finished with the letter C, Albin died in a car accident. He had already drawn up his will and, heartbreakingly, he left me the most beautiful of his guitars.

In September no doubt I'll get back to work, alone (and with so much sorrow, I can tell already), and tackle the letter D.

. . . .

My musical and linguistic activities, and of course Anna's upbringing, occupied my whole life.

IV

Carrying several bags in each arm, I pushed backward through the red curtain that hung in the kitchen doorway. (This curtain, extremely worn today, was woven by Maria's maternal grandmother, who had given it to her as a wedding present.)

A few moments later I opened the freezer door and saw a package of frozen food — a single package — sitting in the exact center of the middle shelf.

This is the unbelievable event to which I referred earlier.

Unbelievable, because I was absolutely certain the freezer had been empty when we'd left for Cologne. Amalia had even defrosted and cleaned it. Empty, definitely empty! Where had this frozen food come from? Who had brought it into my kitchen? Furthermore — and I looked carefully now at the wrapper — the package contained clams. I never buy clams. And as for the brand, Marty Frigor, I'd never even heard of it. I'd never seen it in any store.

I had to face facts: while I was away someone had come into my house and placed a package of Marty Frigor clams in my freezer.

Who? Why?

My first impulse was to be afraid for Anna, as if this mystery threatened her in some way.

I couldn't find the slightest trace of a break-in.

Who had my keys? Amalia. But I just couldn't imagine that Amalia . . . no. Still, she did have my keys hanging in her hallway beneath my name, along with those to the apartments of her various other employers. Could the mysterious delivery person have stolen my keys from her apartment and then gone to my place on Rue Mademoiselle?

Amalia was not leaving for Madrid to visit her parents for another two days. I wanted to set my mind at rest, so I called her and said I would be dropping by — no, it was nothing serious, I'd explain everything when I got there.

I put away my groceries.

Before I went out, I looked up "Marty Frigor" in the phone book. Sure enough, a frozen food store by this name could be found at 6 Rue Scolie in the 5th Arrondissement. It was a wholesale shop and sold only to institutions.

I went to Amalia's on Boulevard Ney. She lived on the ground floor at the rear of a courtyard.

She greeted me with her usual hospitality. I told her my story. Of course she hadn't been to Rue Mademoiselle while I was in Cologne, she told me without the slightest hesitation.

I scanned her apartment while I questioned her. She said she had not been at home Saturday afternoon, and in the summer she left the kitchen window slightly ajar without always remembering to close the window catch.

Could someone have come in through this window, taken

the key, and put it back in place after having used it? The hypothesis made Amalia smile. Nonetheless, as pure hypothesis, she admitted it couldn't be entirely dismissed.

. . . .

The Rue Scolie runs parallel to the Seine and links Boulevard Saint-Maurice to Rue Viviane.

I went through the carriage entrance at number 6, between a seed store and a dressmaker's shop, both of which were closed in August, and crossed a courtyard at the rear of which the Marty Frigor warehouse was located.

A glass door slid open as I approached.

I went in. Countless tubs of frozen food packages were lined up in rows. The place was rather chilly. To my right, some fifteen feet away in a glass office, a man was speaking on the telephone. As soon as he noticed me, he motioned for me to come in and pointed to a chair across from him, as if he had been expecting me.

He hung up the phone. His gaze was candid, gentle, kindly. I invented a story: I was to meet a friend at her house, I was early, I was admiring some of the inner courtyards of this lovely neighborhood to pass the time. When I saw a frozen goods store, I had got it into my head to buy a strawberry pie and bring it to my friend. But I realized now that I was in a wholesale shop.

He confirmed this. Marty Frigor was an American company recently established in France, and it sold only wholesale.

A red notebook lay in front of him open to the last page on which there was writing. He tapped it lightly with his hand:

"Look. The Magnum hotel chain ordered eight thousand items from me. (Tap, tap with his hand again.) The Miraflor factories, six thousand, for their company cafeterias in the North."

He seemed proud of these figures, and happy to chat with someone. I asked him the question that had led me to Rue Scolie in the first place:

"Do you ever sell to individuals?"

"No. Well, yes, once, last week. To my neighbor across the way. But that's a different story. (His index finger ran along the first line of the page.) Sixty packages of clams."

"Sixty packages! That's practically wholesale," I said, smiling.

"A birthday dinner. He's celebrating his birthday tonight."

"May I ask why he got this special treatment?"

"Would you believe he treated me to lunch at the Scolie? We knew each other by sight, we were sitting at neighboring tables, and I had forgotten my checkbook. Afterward, he would not let me pay him back. (With sadness:) The poor man cannot get over his mother's death. What a nice fellow! When he told me his sister adored clams and that he was thinking of buying some for his birthday celebration, I offered . . . (The man gave me a huge smile.) Well, I'm going to offer you your strawberry pie, too! In business, you always have to factor in some loss!"

As I was thanking him, we heard the sound of an engine in the courtyard followed by two little beeps of a horn. The frozen food man got up and asked me to wait for him a minute.

While he was gone, I twisted my neck to read the name on top of the page: Marc Kram.

Albin and I had known a Marc Kram at college; he was a friendly but guarded student who only came to classes when he felt like it. Could this be the same Marc Kram?

Back at home on Rue Mademoiselle, stretched out on my sofa, eyes half closed, I listened to the Croatian guitarist Ana Vidovic (winner of the first prize at the Benicassim competition in ____), who had raised the art of guitar playing to incomparable heights of perfection.

After my lonely dinner, I called Anna and we spoke, as usual, for a long time.

I would have been happy to talk with my daughter for all eternity.

"Till tomorrow, my darling. I'll take you out to dinner then, okay?"

At 8:30 p.m., overcoming my exhaustion, I called Marc Kram. I said my name and asked him if . . . And he was! He was indeed the Marc Kram Albin and I had known when we were students. I told him I had come across his name by chance in the phone book and I hadn't been able to resist calling. He said he was glad. In fact, if I were free, he was giving a party that very evening; it was his birthday. Why not take advantage of the occasion?

I agreed.

Third floor, apartment on the left, all the doors would be open he said before hanging up.

I showered and changed my clothes.

. . . .

Marc was waiting for me.

He was very pained to learn of Albin's death. I was amazed at how clear his memories of Albin and me were.

He led me into his bedroom, where we could be alone. We managed to make our way through the endless corridors of an enormous apartment where groups of guests were wandering about.

A huge living room had been turned into a dance floor.

As I walked through the kitchen, I noticed two bags filled with Marty Frigor products. The name could be read distinctly through the transparent plastic.

We gave each other succinct accounts of our lives. After finishing his studies, Marc had gone on to a political career (a covert one: his name never appeared anywhere). He had become rich when his father died, just as a change in government had left him without a job. But he was happy being unemployed. He was not bored; he was in no hurry to find a new profession.

He talked about his mother's death with difficulty. He was sorry his half-sister, Agathe, was not at the party. He told me about her and said she would have been happy to see me. She had not forgotten me; she had even asked him on several occasions if he had heard from me.

I had not forgotten Agathe either. She had been a mere child at the time, and I had been charmed by her gracefulness and her very blond hair. She was about ten years younger than Marc. Brother and sister had different mothers.

"I too am sorry she's not here," I said.

"Unfortunately, she's not well. Our doctor thinks it's only nerves. But she's very weak. She sleeps all the time. I can't help but worry."

The two of them were going on vacation not far from Paris in two days. Marc hoped the change of scenery and the country air would do Agathe good.

"How I miss her tonight!" he said again. "The clams were for her. Oh, I'm sorry. Have you eaten yet? Would you like something?"

"No, thank you," I said.

He seemed preoccupied.

"You know . . . about those clams . . ."

"What about them?"

"Oh, nothing really, but . . . Something happened that I don't understand. I bought sixty packages. I even counted them again before I put them in the freezer. And today as I was getting everything ready I found only fifty-nine. One package has disappeared. Odd, isn't it?"

"Yes, very odd," I said. "Are you sure?"

"Absolutely."

I struck Marc Kram from my list of suspects . . . and then I had none.

What had happened? Was it possible someone had placed this same missing package in *my* freezer? But who?

Agathe?

The bedroom door opened — people were looking for Marc to say hello, or to introduce him to someone . . .

"Please excuse me. My role as host . . ." he said with a sad smile. "We'll see each other a little later, okay? In the meantime, enjoy the party; dance!"

Dancing was certainly not on my mind.

Since Maria's death, I no longer had any desire of any kind.

Anna was my whole and only life.

With a glass of water in my hand, I entered a small sitting room that was nearly empty. A lone couple was dancing to the sound of distant music. Four other people were chatting in low voices at one end of the room. I sat with my glass at the other end, wondering what to do next.

The four conspirators left the room, followed by the dancing couple — and then a young woman with dark hair arrived.

She sat down. Soon, as if it were the most natural thing in the world, she began talking to me. I answered merely to be polite. She continued speaking, and little by little I was drawn into a conversation that I didn't really want to have.

The young woman's name was Marthe. Like me, she had come from the city of L, where her mother still lived, and had only been in Paris for a year — she had come to study art history. She wanted to become a museum curator. She also painted a bit — self-portraits. She loved the deserted summer city.

I spoke to her mostly about Anna.

The music stopped then started again. Marthe got up and held out her hand to me — and we danced. Against my will? Perhaps. At the time, I couldn't have said. I didn't think; I let myself go.

The dance ended. She stepped back and then she made a tiny gesture with her hand — a sort of tic I had already noticed: head tilted, she gently smoothed her right eyebrow with her right index finger.

Then she smiled at me, pointed to the door, and left the room in a way that made it seem she was headed for the bathroom, say, or for the bar, or to speak to somebody, and that she would be right back.

But she didn't come back.

I looked for her everywhere in the apartment.

She was no longer there. She had left.

Two extraordinary events in the same day!

Was there some secret link between them? Absurdly, I thought there was.

Who was this Marthe?

Marc had no idea. He knew no one who met the description I gave him. Had he invited people whom he'd never met before? No. Of course, some of his guests had brought friends of theirs . . . He had an idea, he said — that is, if I weren't afraid of giving a short speech.

He gathered his guests in the living room and asked for everyone's attention. Overcoming my embarrassment, I described Marthe, her height, her dress, her hair, her beauty, the intensity of her gaze, and even the gesture of smoothing her eyebrow.

But no one had seen her; no one had seen a woman like that at the party.

I gleaned no information, gathered no clues.

. . . .

A little later, Marc and I were together again in his room. Without worrying that he would think I was some kind of womanizer, I said:

"I felt like I was acting against my will; it was as if she had cast a spell on me. Such a strange experience, followed by her strange disappearance . . . I want to know. Can you understand that?"

"Certainly," he said. "Unfortunately, everyone who was supposed to come to the party came; that's all I can tell you. Except my sister, of course."

Except Agathe, his sister . . . On hearing those words, a line of reasoning that seemed flawless came to me: everyone who was supposed to come had come; the only person who knew about the party and who was absent was Agathe; therefore, if Marthe was not a complete stranger who had come by sheer chance to Marc Kram's, well then . . . Marthe could be Agathe in disguise. Did Agathe resemble Marthe? (I didn't dare ask Marc.) Agathe was blond. Still, she could have dyed her hair or worn a wig, cleverly made herself up, come to the party and not have been noticed — and the trick was played.

But what trick? Why would Agathe do such a thing? To speak to me incognito? But why speak to me incognito? And how could she have known I would be at her brother's? Because she was the one who had placed the clams in my freezer and had foreseen that I would embark on an investigation that would lead me to call Marc?

I had no answer as to why someone would undertake such an implausible, risky venture. But perhaps there was one.

I did my best to keep my crazy imaginings at bay, without real success. The vague and menacing distress I had felt in regard to Anna in the afternoon still nagged at me to such an extent that, in spite of myself, I was determined to leave no hypothesis out because I needed to be absolutely certain about everything.

"I'd be very happy to see Agathe again," I said to Marc. "Do you think I could phone her?"

"Of course! She'd be thrilled!"

He wrote her number on a piece of paper. His eagerness surprised me. It was as if he were afraid of being suspected of something . . . but of what? Of being possessive with his sister? Of preventing her from mixing with dangerous men? That was the sense I got.

He handed me the slip of paper.

"I'll tell her you came to the party. I'm supposed to call her after the guests have left, no matter what time it is."

Suddenly his eyes filled with tears.

He pulled himself together, apologized, and spoke to me about his mother, Irène, who had died a year and a half earlier from kidney disease. According to him, it was the doctors who had killed her, not her illness. He was especially infuriated with a famous and very wealthy nephrologist, Dr. Amédée Marquis, an elderly man, short and stocky, with thick gray hair that was too long — he described a veritable monster to me — and who was, he thought, insane, certifiably insane.

He told me the story with details he had as yet revealed to no one, not even to his sister.

I was overcome with compassion. What cruel echoes of suffering his words awoke in my heart!

He placed his hands on my shoulders.

"Thank you for having listened to me, my dear X. And forgive me for complaining to you when I now know what trials you have been through. But I couldn't help myself. To tell you the truth, when you called me earlier tonight, I already knew I would confide in you. I had the urge to do so from the start."

VI

The morning of the next day, August 2, I went to Agathe Kram's at 30 Rue Blanche, a short walk from the high school where she taught Latin and Greek. Taking the chance of waking her, I'd called at 9:00 a.m.

One thing became immediately clear: although she was as remarkably elegant and beautiful as Marthe, Agathe was not Marthe. All the wigs and make-up in the world could not have accomplished such a miraculous transformation. If I'd had any lingering doubts about the matter, they evaporated as soon as she opened the door.

We recognized each other at first glance despite the years that had passed, and were very moved to see each other again.

I asked about her health. She said she felt much better — free from the despondency of the last few days, from the constant and sometimes pressing torpor that had made her fall asleep at any moment and that had distorted her memory. (For example, Sunday morning she had woken up in a different room from the one in which she'd thought she'd fallen asleep.)

I gave her the same succinct life story that I had given her brother: *doleüre et mort*, almost perpetual motion, unfinished dictionary, Anna.

She asked me a thousand little questions about Anna.

"How lucky you are to have such a treasure! Are you going on vacation with her?"

"Yes, at the end of the month. We're going to Spain. And you? Marc told me . . ."

She seemed unenthusiastic (or so I thought) about leaving with her brother the next day in mid-afternoon.

Then, as I was admiring her delicate, shapely hands, she tilted her head and ran her right index finger across her right eyebrow.

"Do you do that often?"

I imitated her so she would know what I was talking about. She smiled.

"No, I don't think so. I don't know."

Hardly two seconds had gone by when another sign appeared to me: I noticed a bit of red thread on her dress. Was it the same red as my kitchen curtain? I sometimes found little bits of thread like that on my own clothing. I picked it off and handed it to her. She looked at it, surprised:

"I don't have any red clothes! Oh, yes, one dress, but I've never worn it. And it's a darker red."

"Perhaps you're a sleepwalker?" I said. "You lead a secret life when you're asleep, and you got this red thread in an apartment other than yours . . . No?"

This time, she laughed outright.

"Not to my knowledge!" she said.

. . . .

In the car, I was subjected to another merciless bout of crazy thoughts. Agathe's fits of languor, the red thread on her clothing, the way she stroked her eyebrow, her forgotten nocturnal wanderings — didn't everything lead me to believe that Marthe the sorceress had hypnotized Agathe (in the street, in a store, anywhere!), taken over her body, substituted her will for Agathe's, and used her to carry out that task on Saturday afternoon, to steal my keys from Amalia's and place a package of Marty Frigor frozen clams in my freezer?

Why? Well — and I touched on this when I thought Agathe was the guilty party — so that what had happened would happen. So that I would be surprised and worried when I returned from Cologne, start an investigation, speak to the Marty Frigor employee, then to Marc Kram, then to Agathe — in a word, so that I would meet Agathe Kram in the end. But why? So that Agathe and I would be brought together, so that Marc's sister would become my new companion and a new mother for Anna? Hadn't Agathe loved me since she was a girl, and hadn't she shown an obsessive interest in Anna? Did nothing hold any secrets for the omniscient Marthe?

While I can't deny that during the drive from Rue Blanche to Rue Mademoiselle I thought that Marthe was fate itself — fate that had decided to get mixed up in human affairs — I must immediately add that I was not entirely convinced by this idea. I was well aware that all the above was merely theoretical, but I allowed myself to go down the dizzying path of this possibility because it had the advantage of explaining, point by point, the series of events that had occurred over the last two days, and this — for want of a better hypothesis — provided me with a certain satisfaction.

Agathe, inhabited by Marthe's spirit last Saturday afternoon!

And Agathe would have kept a trace of Marthe's foreign presence — the tic, the smoothing of her right eyebrow . . .

VII

I picked Anna up at about 5:00 in the evening and we headed for Rue de Rome. I parked in front of Monnier's bookstore, where I had ordered a very old, anonymous work on musical transcription. The saleswoman told me they had received it that very morning.

From there we walked to La Flute de Pan, where I had ordered the sheet music for a harpsichord suite that in fact I wanted to transcribe for the guitar. (Every project of this kind reminded me of Albin de Vil, and my heart was heavy with grief.) Again a saleswoman told me they had received it that very morning.

We went back to the car; Anna skipped beside me, laughing, carefree, looking at everything around her with the curiosity of a small animal.

I told her that soon she would have a new friend, Agathe, the sister of a college friend, Marc.

Finally, my musical errands took us to a record store (I had been one of its first customers) on the Boulevard des Italiens, across from the enormous Crédit Lyonnais building. I wanted to buy an album, one of my favorites, to give to Agathe. I couldn't find it on the shelf, but Mathilde, the Sicilian record dealer, came to help me and unearthed two copies as if by magic. Without thinking, I bought them both. Did I do this so I could give one to Marthe as well, if I were destined to see her again one day? I believe so.

I asked Anna if she wanted to take a stroll before dinner in the Luxembourg Garden. She did. She never said no to me. She had a lovely smile playing on her closed lips, looked me straight in the eye, and nodded with a small, lively movement that made her brown locks quiver.

We had been strolling down the Garden paths for less than five minutes when I noticed Marthe in the distance.

She was sitting on a bench, reading.

She closed her book and saw me in turn.

Her face lit up with surprise and joy.

Anna leaned into me.

"Is that Agathe?"

"No, sweetheart, that's Marthe! But I did meet her at Agathe's brother's house. She's also very nice, and I told her a lot about you."

Marthe put her book in her bag and stood up. I introduced the two of them. Anna took to Marthe immediately. I knew my daughter well; she was always delightful, but she did not easily place her trust in people.

She trusted Marthe at once.

Had Marthe bewitched her as she had bewitched Agathe and me? In any case, her eyes shone with pure goodness as they rested on Anna.

"I wonder if any other little girl has a watch as lovely as yours!" she said. "Birthday present?"

Anna let out a contented little laugh and pointed to the gift-giver.

We sat on the bench. I waited for Marthe to offer some explanation, and she did so almost immediately. She asked me to forgive her for the previous evening. She had in fact been heading to the bathroom, where she had felt faint — no, nothing serious; according to the doctor she'd gone to see, it was nothing but nerves. She had returned to the room where we'd been dancing, but I'd already left. She didn't have the energy to look for me in the vast apartment. She'd felt suffocated and had hurried home.

She confessed that she'd thought to call Marc Kram to ask him about me because she was eager to see me again. She would surely have called him by the end of the day. The only reason she hadn't done so already was because she was embarrassed — yes, embarrassed; she'd hesitated because she would have had to lie . . .

She felt very lonely in Paris, so sometimes, for want of anything better to do, or as a game, when she passed an apartment from which she could hear the sounds of a rather large party, she would go inside and mingle with the guests. That's how she had wound up the previous evening on the third floor of 5 Rue Scolie.

I believed her. And, on reflection, the fact that no one had noticed her was not all that surprising.

The sun was low in the sky. A warm breeze began to blow.

"Anna and I were just about to go out to dinner. Would you care to join us?"

"With pleasure!"

"Anna, is it alright with you if . . ."

"With pleasure!"

They laughed.

Marthe took Anna by the hand and we left the Garden.

In the car, I gave Marthe one of the two albums I'd bought.

"You can tell that I also intended to see you again," I said.
She smiled.

"It's a perfect choice," she said as she looked at it.

She slipped it in her bag and kissed me, then kissed Anna
so she wouldn't be jealous, and finally Anna and I kissed as
we all laughed again.

During dinner, Marthe's tic appeared twice — that same
dainty gesture accompanied by a somewhat melancholy expression that I had seen Agathe perform that very morning.

The meal was sublime. We ate in a *crêperie* on Rue Moselle
that had been recommended to me by the Michelangelis, who
were great connoisseurs in matters of food.

Agathe and I had agreed she would call me when she returned
from Saint-Rometz. But before leaving the restaurant, on an
impulse I went downstairs to the pay phones and called her. I
asked her if she would be kind enough to meet me before she
left the following afternoon. She readily agreed.

. . . .

It was 9:30 at night when I turned onto Avenue Marguerite.

From a distance I could see Lorima putting out a last bag
of trash atop a bin already filled to bursting.

I parked. Anna and Marthe said good-bye to each other.

"See you soon, my little Anna!" said Marthe.

"Yes . . ."

"As soon as possible?"

"Yes!"

I walked Anna into the house, made some small talk with Maureen, and left.

The trash bin on the sidewalk was visible from the Maxima. A ray of light fell on the bag that Lorima had placed there, and through the transparent blue plastic I could read the word "children" written in large gothic type on a brochure of some kind.

Marthe lived in a three-room apartment overlooking a courtyard (planted with trees and flowers) on the fourth floor of a building on Rue Bernarde, near the Madeleine Church.

She used one of the three rooms as her painting studio. I didn't know if it was out of self-consciousness or modesty, but she didn't want to show me the ten or so self-portraits she had painted that year. I insisted, but in vain (another time, she said), and the door to the studio remained closed while I was there.

We would have wanted to listen to the album I had given her, but her stereo was being repaired so we couldn't.

For the third time in less than twenty-four hours I was led to recount my life story, and I gave Marthe the most detailed narrative of all. I told her about events I had not previously confided to anyone (not even to my dear Albin), including my in-laws' madness when they suspected me of having murdered Maria.

I arrived at the most recent past: the trip to Cologne with Anna, the Marty Frigor mystery, my investigation, Marc, his sister Agathe; the words flowed effortlessly out of my mouth (whose extraordinary resemblance to Anna's Marthe had indeed noticed). And I did not hide the conclusions I had come to, according to which everything fell perfectly into place if one imagined that she, Marthe, had pulled all the strings ("including the red one," she joked, playing along with me) — if, in other words, one assumed that she were the very incarnation of fate, or of death, its faithful servant, or of some hybrid figure that was a mix of the two, fate and death, according to an infinite combination of possible proportions.

She smiled.

"Your theory is perfect. 'Death, fate's faithful servant . . .' Tired of being nothing but a spirit, I wanted to incarnate myself in the body of a mortal woman at the risk . . . at the risk of meeting you," she said softly.

We kissed once, and then a thousand times.

What kind of love united us?

Never did I have the sense that I was being unfaithful to the memory of Maria, or betraying Anna's trust, or Agathe's. And when I left Marthe I knew — we both knew — that physical desire would no longer be a part of our relationship.

This was yet another mystery solved today (today!), like all the others.

IX

I set the perpetual motion machine in motion again; it had stopped (something that never would have happened had Anna been there), and I was pleased to see the seascape light up and come to life within its aquarium — the fleecy waves, the shadows gliding along the shore — without any part of the system running on batteries or connected to an electric outlet of any kind. The description of my father's invention had enchanted Marc, Agathe, and Marthe, so I wrote to Maurice de Vil to ask him to send out three aquariums of the same model as mine when he came back from vacation on August 21: one to Marc Kram at 6 Rue Scolie, another to Agathe Kram at 30 Rue Blanche, and a third to Marthe L at 9 Rue Bernarde.

They would receive them before the end of the month.

Then I showered, changed, and went to meet Agathe as planned at 11:00 a.m. at the Malaquais, on the Quai Malaquais next to the École des Beaux-Arts.

I gave her her album. She thanked me and kissed me with childlike joy. I had been truly inspired, she said: it was sheer chance that she hadn't already bought it herself!

She felt much better. Her languorous drowsiness had vanished — in fact, I found her on the contrary full of nervous energy, anxious even. As our conversation continued, I became more and more convinced that her impending trip lay at the root of her anxiety.

"I'm happy to be here with you. You did the right thing by calling me last night."

I thought of the phone call I had made to her out of the blue from the restaurant . . . Under Marthe's influence, under the effect of some hypnotic suggestion of hers?

Agathe went on:

"And I would be happy to meet Anna. You've made me want to get to know her."

"That's easy," I said. "Whenever you'd like. I've already mentioned you to her."

"When I get back from vacation?"

After that vacation that was obsessing her, that seemed to be a barrier between her and life?

"Will you be gone long?"

"I don't know."

"The whole month?"

She hesitated.

"No, about two weeks. Even less if I'm too bored."

She and Marc were hardly going far from Paris — in fact, they were traveling to Saint-Rometz, near Chartres, to stay in a chateau that had been converted into a hotel, near Aunay-sous-Auneau, the famous medieval village where a few miles away was a psychiatric hospital, the Antoine de La Salle Institute, where mentally ill patients who were considered beyond help were cared for in the most humane way. (I knew this because a friend of a friend had been institutionalized there two or three years earlier.)

The Saint-Rometz chateau, Agathe told me, was an unbelievably luxurious establishment, both a hotel and a kind of family resort.

What she said next surprised me:

"It's been alleged that the chateau harbors a sect and that Y, the owner, is the sect's leader. But that's nothing but slander. Marc used to work with Y, and he knows the rumors are false. Saint-Rometz is open to families — children are welcome, and the guests can meet for meals, games, and walks if they want to, but that's it. There's nothing evil going on there!"

It was as if she were on the defensive or trying unsuccessfully to convince herself that Saint-Rometz was not the heart of hell. Was this young woman, so pure in body and soul, afraid of being close to her brother in the chateau, afraid of the complicity between her brother and Y, the leader of the accursed ceremonies and a man whom Marc had frequented during his brief political career that was shrouded in mystery?

When it came time to say good-bye, I held Agathe in my arms. And — my own words surprised me — I asked her if she would like to accompany Anna and me to the little village in southern Spain where we were going at the end of the month.

Incredulous, with a radiant smile, she enthusiastically answered yes.

. . . .

I spent the afternoon with my daughter. First I bought her clothes, books, and games that would be useful or amusing for her at Saint-Haynaut-le-Haut. (Not that she needed any of it, as you can imagine; but making her happy overjoyed me, and I would have offered her the entire city on a silver platter.) Then, at 5:00, we went to Marthe's. She had invited us to come between 5:00 and 6:00; she had told me on the phone, without going into any more detail, that she was busy before and after. Of one thing I was sure: she was eager for our company.

And Anna was eager for hers as well. She literally did not leave Marthe's side the entire time. Marthe had prepared a delicious afternoon snack, and for a few moments I was worry-free and at peace.

As we were leaving, Marthe asked me for news of Agathe.

"She's fine," I said. "She and her brother are in Saint-Rometz, near Chartres."

"Saint-Rometz? Y's sect?"

"Is it really a sect?" I asked, amazed.

"I don't know. It could be."

"Is that what you heard, or . . ."

"Yes, through a friend whose brother is a journalist. A year ago, he wrote an article on Saint-Rometz, but his paper wouldn't publish it. There was no proof and they were afraid of a lawsuit."

. . . .

Late that night, lying on my couch, I read and reread the sheet music I had bought at La Flute de Pan so that I almost knew it by heart.

Saint-Rometz, Y, a sect!

Then I went into my study, where Albin and I had so often worked together.

Three entire walls were lined with dictionaries from different eras. On a Spanish table made of dark wood lay the manuscript of our unfinished etymological dictionary.

I pulled back a velvet drape, thick and pleated like a theater curtain. My eleven guitars appeared, twelve counting Albin's, all very valuable instruments.

I selected one and began to play the first measures of the harpsichord suite.

And so Wednesday came to an end.

X

The next day, Thursday, August 4, at 3:00 p.m., I went to see Dr. Luis Moreno in his enormous office on Avenue Marceau. I told him the story I already mentioned on page 7 of this narrative, about my cousin Michèle, who had been saved by Suig and Moreno in L, my native city.

Luis Moreno Jr. was struck by the coincidence, and his eyes became misty for a moment at the mention of his dead father.

My blood tests were puzzling but not alarming, he said after a short while. The myelogram would most likely detect a small anomaly of no consequence, and that would be that. I was to come by the next day at 6:30 p.m. and he would have the results.

I got undressed and underwent the exam that Hervé Mateau had described to me. Moreno removed a few pieces of bone marrow by sticking a long needle in my sternum.

Ow, oohh, ow!

Despite the anesthesia, it was not pleasant.

. . . .

42

When I got home, I found a breathless message from Maureen Michelangeli: Anna, our Anna, whom I loved more than life . . .

Anna had been kidnapped in Parc Monceau after her nap while she was taking a walk with Lorima.

I got back in my car and raced to Avenue Marguerite.

A woman had found Lorima lying in the grass, a wad of cloth under her nose, still dizzy from the sleeping drug in which the cloth had been soaked. Lorima remembered nothing other than that she had been attacked from behind while Anna was happily playing, not far from her but out of her sight, and that she had immediately lost consciousness.

And Anna had disappeared.

I hurried to the park. The police were searching the area, questioning the people strolling through the park and making other arrangements by telephone.

They questioned me as well.

An hour after I got there, a first, terrible assessment could be made: Anna had indeed been kidnapped; there were no witnesses, no possible suspect, no specific leads.

Kidnapped! But by whom, my God, by whom? By an ordinary criminal who knew we were wealthy and who would ask for a ransom from the Michelangelis and me?

I called Marthe and told her the awful news.

Was she less surprised than she should have been? I managed to put that question — and many others — out of my mind and said her presence would be a comfort to me.

"In fact, I wanted to see you. I was just about to call you."

We decided to meet at my place on Rue Mademoiselle.

I sobbed the whole ride home.

XI

A flyer was sticking out of my mailbox; I could read the word "children" written on it in gothic letters. I grabbed it. It was a brochure (like the one in the Michelangelis' trash can on Tuesday evening? Yes, definitely.), put out by an association I'd never heard of: United Family.

While I was waiting for Marthe, I skimmed it. The goal of United Family was to help people who wanted to adopt a child go through the often discouraging steps they needed to take to do so. In the penultimate paragraph of the brochure, it said that the association could help in a variety of "perfectly legal" ways — as if it were necessary to specify this! As if they thought it extraordinary not to be at the head of a ghastly ring of child traffickers!

Marthe rang the doorbell.

She took me in her arms and whispered words of hope.

"Why did you want to see me?" I asked.

She hesitated, then said she had managed that morning to get a copy of the article on Saint-Rometz about which she had told me.

"Do you have it on you?" I asked.

She took it out of her bag. In exchange I gave her the United Family brochure.

The author of the article, Marc T, described life at Saint-Rometz in nightmare terms. If children were so welcome at Saint-Rometz, he wrote, it was in order to indoctrinate them and to mold future followers. It was also to have them participate in dreadful nocturnal ceremonies — I tremble at the thought of repeating what I read — that could even lead to human sacrifice.

No proof. The journalist interpreted coincidences, associated clues, made logical deductions. He almost had a witness — a young man who, alas, was killed in a car accident the day Marc T was to take down his testimony. A suspicious accident? Marc T implied as much.

Anna's kidnapping had thrown me into a world of terror, and I was beset by a flood of dreadful suppositions. My face must have changed, because Marthe became worried: what was happening to me?

I expressed my fears to her: Did Maureen and Maurice Michelangeli hate me, and did they secretly hate my daughter Anna, more than I ever could have imagined, so much so that they had delivered her up to United Family, an organization that in fact had received a request for a child from Marc Kram, who was trying to please Y? And wasn't Anna being held at this very moment in the Saint-Rometz chateau, exposed to the gravest of dangers?

Marthe stroked my hair and my feverish cheek. My in-laws, like many other people, she said, had simply found an advertisement that they then tossed in the trash. And as for Marc T, he was only following the dictates of his profession: he took pleasure in terrifying his readers and making a mountain out of a molehill. There was obviously no reason to be alarmed.

Surely she was right. But I didn't calm down. Worse, I began to suspect her . . . Hadn't she slipped the brochure into my mailbox? Did this Marc T really exist? Hadn't she written the article herself — and perhaps even made up the brochure?

Wasn't she in fact tightening the grip in which she'd held me from the start?

No, I screamed to myself, no! Marthe was good, loving, caring; to believe otherwise was sheer insanity.

I told her I would die if I didn't do something. But what? I was obsessed by a crazy idea. Marthe tried to dissuade me from carrying it out, but she failed. And because she wanted to support me, she accompanied me.

Before we left, I called the Michelangelis, then the police. Nothing.

. . . .

In the middle of the night, Marthe and I broke into the offices of United Family at 20 Rue de Milan. Luck was with us: the key to my own apartment opened the door!

We discovered two large rooms, dirty and badly furnished. There was a poster on the wall that indicated we were indeed in the organization's headquarters. Marthe headed straight for a dusty, decrepit computer and sat down in front of it. After a few key strokes, which I found extremely deft, a list of names appeared on the screen; there was nothing that specified what the list was of.

. . . .

A, B, C, D, E, F, G, H, I, J, K . . .

. . . .

Under the letter K, we saw the name Marc Kram.

So there *was* a link between him and the organization!

No, Marthe said, no. Marc's name on the list didn't mean a thing. In fact, she remarked, everyone on the list lived in the 5th Arrondissement, and the names had simply been grouped together for the mailing.

But a shadow of a doubt had crept into my mind.

We left, locking the door behind us.

Overcome with grief, completely unnerved and plagued by a thousand suspicions, I suddenly longed to be alone.

Marthe understood.

Her tic had disappeared, or else I just didn't notice it anymore.

I took her back to Rue Bernarde.

She told me she would not leave her apartment and that I shouldn't hesitate to call her whenever I felt the need.

She would be at my disposal.

She'd planned to visit her mother sometime in August, but she would put off the trip as long as necessary.

XII

After several hours of insomnia and mental torture (hadn't Marthe gone alone to Rue de Milan earlier that day, to United Family, an association that hardly seemed to exist, so she could enter Marc Kram's name in the computer and turn the wheel of fate forward a few notches?), I called the police and then the Michelangelis one more time.

Nothing, still nothing . . .

I told Maureen I would come to Avenue Marguerite later that morning.

Were my in-laws to blame for Anna's disappearance?

No! No!

Still, I needed to be absolutely sure. If I could see them, observe them, scrutinize them, I thought that . . .

But nothing came of it. I didn't know how to interpret their silence or their evasive, even hostile, glances. I had to be honest enough to imagine that they were simply numb with grief; or perhaps at times they were tempted to turn their apprehension and anxiety against a scapegoat — against me, the person who had brought misfortune on both their daughter and grand-

I thanked him. He seemed pleased to have helped me.

The small hotel was magnificent, as magnificent as the village itself.

We went in.

My heart was beating wildly.

The receptionist, a middle-aged woman, didn't ask us any questions. Why? Was that the rule? She nodded to me in a friendly way, and smiled at Marthe. As if she already knew her? Yes, as if she already knew her, as if she had already seen her at the hotel! That's why no questions were asked!

The elevator was in use. I took the stairs and Marthe followed.

Second floor. We were in front of room 24; it faced the stairs. Was the door locked?

In an almost authoritarian tone of voice, Marthe told me to open it.

I did.

The room was splendid, crowded with furniture, wall-hangings, and other objects.

I went in.

Anna was lying fully clothed on a large bed.

For a fraction of a second I thought she was dead, but she was sleeping and, after that same fraction of a second, she opened her eyes — intact, radiant, alive.

She had taken a nap, as she did every day in the summer, and she was just waking up.

As soon as she saw me, she tapped her watch with her index finger to let me know that it was about time I had showed up, and then she held her arms out to me. I ran to her and kissed her with so much passion that she laughed.

She wasn't at all surprised by my presence, or by Marthe's.

This was the irrefutable proof that Marthe had engineered the whole thing from the start, the entire story in every little detail!

What tales had she invented after drugging Lorima in order to drag Anna all the way to this hotel so that, twenty-four hours later, Anna would greet us as if it were the most natural thing in the world?

I turned to Marthe.

"Why?" I asked her.

And then I noticed something that made my blood run cold: Marthe was watching our effusions with perfect indifference; her gaze was empty, as if the Marthe I knew had shed her mortal skin.

"You know why," she said in a toneless voice. "So that you and Anna would find yourselves together in this room today . . ."

I didn't have time to think about what she had just said, or to question her, or to act in any way at all: I heard strange noises — a cry perhaps — and in a purely instinctive reflex I buried Anna's face in the sheets. All of a sudden the door burst open and a hideous-looking monster stormed in. At first I thought it was a woman because of the long white hair surrounding its head, but it was a man — Amédée Marquis! He was short and corpulent, with a bloodstained nose and a grimace of hatred contorting his lips — and he was brandishing a gun (I learned later that he had stolen it from a policeman, with a strength that was increased tenfold by his madness)!

Suddenly he stood still. He paid no attention to Marthe, or

else he didn't see her, and he started to point his weapon at Anna and me.

Offendre ou deffendre; I could not hesitate: the only thing to do was to protect Anna with my body. I lay on top of her and held her tightly as if I were trying to make her disappear into me, and then I waited for the shot.

There was a moment of terrible silence.

I turned my head, attempting to see.

My gaze met Marthe's. Her face changed instantly — she became Marthe again! — her eyes lit up and her features contorted with the inner battle she was waging.

Amédée Marquis was about to fire.

The shot rang out.

In a single leap Marthe threw herself between Amédée Marquis and the bed where I held Anna in my arms. The bullet hit her in the forehead and she collapsed to the ground.

Once again I could see Amédée Marquis, and once again he took aim at us.

The sound of voices and hurried footsteps filled the stairwell.

A second blast made the room tremble.

But we were not hit. The hour of our death had passed thanks to Marthe's sacrifice.

The shot had not been fired by Amédée Marquis. Someone had fired at him from the stairwell. He fell forward, dead, his neck covered in blood.

Our savior was the homely, smiling policeman whom I had asked for directions, and again he gave me a sort of smile.

In an instant the hotel was crawling with people.

I called the Michelangelis: everything was going to work out, everything was fine, our child had not been kidnapped, I would explain it all to them.

XIV

In the hours that followed, my only concern was to minimize in Anna's mind the horror we had just lived through in the Hôtel de la Fontaine.

And I think I managed to do so, thanks to my skill and to a predisposition of Anna's own temperament (to which I already alluded and whose true nature still remained unknown to me).

I'm sure she didn't see anything. We left room 24 with her face pressed against my chest — and she saw nothing. What she learned about the events came from the story I told her about them with the intention of sparing her young imagination.

How, though, could I hide the fact that Marthe was no longer alive, and that the creature from hell who had fatally injured her had had to be shot down?

I felt a vast and hopeless sorrow for Marthe, and a boundless confusion about the mystery I had witnessed.

But the joy of kissing Anna overpowered everything.

How much cunning and how many lies did it take to explain to the police, out of Anna's earshot, the series of coincidences and misunderstandings after which I had finally recovered my daughter, who I had thought had been kidnapped, in Aunay-sous-Auneau!

I pride myself on having managed to do so with flawless virtuosity: "Anna?" a close friend had told me moments before. "Why, she's sleeping like an angel at the Hôtel de la Fontaine!" This friend had accompanied me to the hotel, and there . . .

I told them the little I knew about Marthe, her address, her work, her mother in L. (What sad news would soon batter that poor woman — just when she was expecting her daughter's visit! I decided to call her one day, to try to console her just a little — and to ask her, if I dared, for one of her daughter's self-portraits, whichever she wanted to give me, as a souvenir of my love for her.)

Unbearably, Marthe had not died instantly.

After my conversation with the police, and while one of the hotel employees was serving a strawberry soda to Anna, I exchanged a few words with Marin Riéra, the doctor who had examined Marthe. Her brain was damaged beyond repair, but a trace of life was still circulating through her. She was going to be taken to his emergency room in the small hospital in Auneau. Could we hope for a miracle? Alas, he told me, we could not. She would never regain consciousness and would die in a matter of hours.

I asked him to let me know when Marthe . . .

He promised he would.

I would have liked to hold Marthe's hand until the very end, but there was Anna to think of. I had to take care of Anna.

I sat down again in front of her, fighting back sobs, even

managing to smile when she made a little gurgling sound as she took her last swallow.

. . . .

We left the hotel.

On the outskirts of the village, I saw a sign that said "Chateau de Saint-Rometz." I slowed down and said to Anna, the words coming on their own:

"Shall we take a little detour? Shall we go to Saint-Rometz?"

I must have wanted to distract her. No doubt I also hoped that Agathe would return to Paris with us, and that we'd all have dinner together that evening . . .

It turned out to be the right idea.

Anna raised her head from my shoulder and looked at me: "Yes! Why?"

"To say hello to Agathe. She's on vacation in the chateau. But whatever you want, my angel . . ."

Yes, whatever my angel wanted, and she wanted to go.

After a few minutes on a pleasant little country road (where we stopped after rounding a curve to let three rabbits take their time crossing), we reached the chateau with its towers — a structure from a bygone era deposited in the middle of nowhere like a stage set.

We entered the building.

It seemed to me the most peaceful and least criminal place on earth.

A receptionist with a German accent informed me that Ms. Kram had cut short her stay and had left the hotel that very afternoon. And Mr. Kram? Yes, he was there. He had not budged from his room. I was intrigued. I hesitated and then asked her to let him know we were there.

Marc received us in his room, on the top floor of the north-west tower, from which there was an unobstructed view of the surrounding countryside.

He marveled at Anna's beauty and stroked her hair.

He didn't seem unduly surprised by our visit, lost as he was in his own thoughts; and by the way he immediately talked to me about Agathe's departure, one would have thought that his relationship with his sister was a normal subject of conversation between us, that I knew all its ins and outs, even its deepest secrets. Hardly had they arrived at Saint-Rometz, he said, that they realized to what extent the idea of vacationing together had been a mistake. They had talked the night away and, after lunch, Agathe had returned to Paris. They parted calmly, with the confidence that they would now be free from the torment that had ravaged them for so long.

This is what Mark confessed to me.

Only then did he ask me more about our trip to Aunay. I was about to carry out the plan I intended to use to answer this question so that Anna would not have to suffer through the story of the fatal episode, when chance came to my rescue: she had had a lot to drink during the day and she needed to go to the bathroom.

I quickly gave Marc a simplified version of the facts, one that Anna herself could have recounted: I had entrusted my daughter to a good friend for a day, and this friend and I were about to kiss her as she woke from her nap at the Hôtel de la Fontaine when . . .

I told him how Amédée Marquis had died, after killing Marthe.

Marc did not care a whit about Amédée Marquis's fate. But between the thought of his mother and his amazement at the coincidence — Marquis institutionalized, and so close to Saint-Rometz! — he was deeply distressed.

He rested his hand on my shoulder.

"How hard you must be taking the loss of your friend!" he said.

I whispered yes, it was hard. We were both on the verge of tears.

. . . .

Anna retreated into sleep during the drive on the highway. Since nothing other than illness could make her sleep in the afternoon outside of her naptime, I pictured with pain and tenderness her small soul fighting against the ghosts that were assailing it.

Some five or six miles outside of Paris, a large butterfly flew into the windshield of the Maxima: a dull thud, spots of thick yellowish liquid, bloody streaks . . . I turned my eyes away for a moment. When I looked again, I no longer saw a thing — the windshield was clear, as if the butterfly had managed to reassemble the thousand fragments of its pulverized body and take wing again.

. . . .

At exactly 6:30 p.m. I rang the bell at Luis Moreno's. He was thrilled to see Anna. (In the hospital, he said, he mostly tended to children.) He reassured me about my test results — not the slightest problem, the bone marrow biopsy had revealed nothing abnormal — but he told me why he had been puzzled: my low hemoglobin levels were a meaningless blip, a unique medical case of effect without cause. I realized that he might have been more worried during my first visit than he had let on — but, as I said, at no time was I afraid.

And then Anna and I left.

At 7:45 I parked on Avenue Marguerite.

Never before had time spent with the Michelangelis been so cordial and so intimate. Not only were their suspicions about my having had a hand in their daughter's death no longer anything but a memory, but that evening I felt as if that memory itself were finally beginning to fade.

I told them my made-up tale.

First I alluded to a dark incident that I would recount to them under different circumstances, suggesting with a gesture and a facial expression that I wanted to spare Anna.

As for the rest . . .

I had warned Anna before we got there that she wasn't to be surprised by what I would tell her grandparents. I would explain everything to her later, soon, and she would understand. In the meantime, it would be our secret. Did she agree?

Our secret! Her eyes shone, and she signaled her agreement to me with the loveliest smile in the world.

And so, as for the rest, "How much cunning and how many lies did it take to explain the series of coincidences and misunderstandings after which I had finally recovered our child, who we thought had been kidnapped, in Aunay-sous-Auneau!"

But nothing existed beyond their joy at Anna's homecoming: as I was losing myself in my fabrications, Maureen, Maurice, and Lorima were smothering her with kisses.

The Michelangelis would go by themselves to Saint-Haynaut-le-Haut, or else they wouldn't go at all. They would be happy to leave Anna with me for as long as I wanted. After what had happened, they respected and approved of my desire to be near my daughter at every moment.

XV

A message from Agathe was waiting for me when I got back to Rue Mademoiselle.

I returned her call at once.

Her brother had told her about our visit to Saint-Rometz. She asked me a few questions (who, for example, was Marthe?) and said she was very eager to see Anna and me.

"Anna is also very eager to see you. And so am I. Will you come to dinner with us? I have clams in my freezer and Marc told me that you like them. And I have a delicious strawberry pie for dessert."

Yes, she exclaimed, she would come! Around 9:00?

I asked her to be discreet in front of Anna about the events of the day.

. . . .

The heat was oppressive. I opened the French doors that led to the balcony and its dwarf trees.

Anna seemed overexcited to me.

We were quick to shower, change our clothes, and set the

table in the kitchen, which was cooler than the rest of the apartment.

Then we went to sit on the black leather sofa. Anna put on some music — Ana Vidovic (for me, she said, holding up the album cover and smiling her pure smile of a goddess) and Juanito Valderrama, to whom I listened, to my surprise, with less sorrow than usual.

Anna looked at her watch and couldn't sit still. I suggested she tidy up her room, which she kept in such disorder that Amalia could never manage to contain it. She agreed. She got up, so beautiful in the red dress I had given to her on Wednesday and that she was wearing for the first time.

She didn't get a chance to do much tidying: two minutes later, the bell rang.

Agathe had brought us flowers and candy. Anna and Agathe kissed, shyly.

Blond Agathe was metamorphosed; she seemed to be a new person, her face open and relaxed despite the circumstances.

She was dazzled by my apartment. I would really have liked to have asked her: "You truly don't remember a thing? The freezer? The red curtain?" Was it in fact possible to believe that she had entered the apartment one night in a trance, bringing into my kitchen the clams that would soon . . .

Still, it was the absolute truth. That was exactly what had happened.

I showed her my study with its Spanish furniture, the twelve guitars, the dictionaries, and in the small sitting room I had her admire the aquarium and its self-sufficient mechanism that allowed the sun to shine on the treetops and the ocean to wet the sand with its waves — and I told her she and Marc would both receive a similar one at the end of August.

But not Marthe, alas!

The wheel was turning. The rubber-coated balls were going up and down.

But I hadn't restarted it since Wednesday.

What was this new mystery?

The telephone rang.

I knew who was calling, and I knew why. I went to the living room to answer it.

It was indeed Marin Riéra, the doctor, true to his word.

"Your friend has just died," he said. "I'm at her side and . . . (His voice changed:) No, she's opening her eyes! (His voice returned to a whisper:) No, the poor thing is really . . ."

He interrupted himself as if he couldn't find the right word.

"Dead?" I asked.

"Excuse me?"

"Is she dead?"

"I don't understand. Is she what?"

"Didn't you just tell me that she was dead?"

After a moment, he repeated:

"Excuse me, I don't understand . . ."

Maybe our connection wasn't good. I thanked him and hung up.

I went back to Agathe and Anna.

"Anna, sweetheart, could you go tidy up your room some

more so that Agathe can see it nice and clean? I'll show her the rest of the apartment and then we'll come, okay?"

A bit surprised but conciliatory, gracious, and smiling with her close-lipped smile, Anna left the room in a whirl of brown curls and red fabric, waving good-bye with exaggerated gestures.

XVI

"I just learned of the death of Marthe L," I said to Agathe.

She stared wide-eyed.

"What? What was that word?"

"Her death . . ."

"Excuse me? Her 'death?'"

She seemed not to understand. For a moment I thought she was playing a game of some kind — but no, not at all.

"She's dead. 'Dead.' You know the word, don't you?"

Agathe looked startled. She raised her hand to her forehead, about to stroke her eyebrow with her index finger, but then stopped.

"Honestly, no, I don't."

I took her gently by the shoulder.

"Come," I said.

First Marin Riéra, now Agathe . . .

I fought back my fear.

We went into my study.

I grabbed a dictionary and held it out to her.

"Look. 'Death,' *d, e, a, t, h.*"

She opened the dictionary, found the right page, ran her eyes over it — and her face lit up with triumphant and childish sincerity when she turned the book to face me:

"See!"

. . . .

I understood in the deepest part of my being.

Even if I could have gathered together everyone on earth, no one could have comprehended my words anymore.

By dying, Marthe . . .

But then, what was the status of the planet since the hour of her death? Where were Maria, Amédée Marquis, Marc's mother, Irène, Luis Moreno's father, Juan Valderrama, my own parents, and Marthe herself? Where had all the dead, present and past, gone? Had they been lost to oblivion? Had they never existed? And how would people recount their history from now on, the histories of their families, their countries, or the history of the world?

And, when September came, was I supposed to write in my own dictionary the history of a word that no longer existed?

I was overwhelmed by an endless stream of questions.

One of them haunted me especially. By her words and through our union, Marthe had made me the guardian of the secret. And I was the only one to have knowledge of our new immortality . . . But would this unique, unbelievable, supernatural knowledge remain in me? Or would it fade like a dream when I awoke the next day, or in a few weeks — or in a few seconds?

My blood ran cold.

I decided to write down the story of what had happened to me on the first of August in the year _ _ _ _ — quickly, as quickly as possible, now, immediately! — so that I would never forget, and so that the story could be revealed to others should one day it become as mysterious to me as it was to them.

. . . .

Agathe was waiting for me, frozen in the same position, holding the open dictionary out to me.

. . . .

From her lovely, delicate hands I take the book, and I look.

Breinigsville, PA USA
28 February 2011
256598BV00001B/1/P

9 780803 224414